-My Family-
My Military Mom

by Claudia Harrington
illustrated by Zoe Persico

Looking Glass Library

An Imprint of Magic Wagon
abdopublishing.com

For Ken, Tess, Gretchen & Emmett, who make my heart beat wildly. With special thanks to Ted Brass. —CH

To my new Bright Group family for believing in me and helping me make my dreams come true. —ZP

abdopublishing.com

Published by Magic Wagon, a division of ABDO, PO Box 398166, Minneapolis, Minnesota 55439. Copyright © 2016 by Abdo Consulting Group, Inc. International copyrights reserved in all countries. No part of this book may be reproduced in any form without written permission from the publisher. Looking Glass Library™ is a trademark and logo of Magic Wagon.

Printed in the United States of America, North Mankato, Minnesota.
052015
092015

THIS BOOK CONTAINS
RECYCLED MATERIALS

Written by Claudia Harrington
Illustrated by Zoe Persico
Edited by Heidi M.D. Elston
Designed by Candice Keimig

Library of Congress Cataloging-in-Publication Data

Harrington, Claudia, 1957- author.
  My military mom / by Claudia Harrington ; illustrated by Zoe Persico.
     pages cm. -- (My family)
  Summary: Lenny follows Connor for a school project and learns about his life with a military mom.
  ISBN 978-1-62402-106-0
1. Children of military personnel--Juvenile fiction. 2. Parent and child--Juvenile fiction. 3. Families--Juvenile fiction. [1. Children of military personnel--Fiction. 2. Parent and child--Fiction. 3. Family life--Fiction. 4. Youths' art.] I. Persico, Zoe, 1993- illustrator. II. Title.
  PZ7.1.H374Mq 2016
  [E]--dc23
                                                    2015002678

"Please welcome our new friend, Connor," said Miss Fish.

"Hi, Connor," said the class.

When the last bell rang, Miss Fish handed Lenny the class camera. "Connor is Student of the Week, so you'll be going home with him today."

"Great!" said Lenny. **Click!**

"How do you get home?" asked Lenny.

"My dad's meeting us today. He didn't want me getting lost the first day." Connor made a goofy face, and both boys laughed.

"Dad!" said Connor when they
burst outside.
Connor's dad scooped him up
in a big bear hug. **Click!**

"This is Lenny," said Connor.
"Nice to meet an ace reporter," said Connor's dad as he shook Lenny's hand.
"Thanks," said Lenny.

When they'd walked several blocks,
Connor pointed. "That's it. Right, Dad?"
"That's affirmative, soldier,"
said Connor's dad.
Click!

"Why does your dad call you soldier?" asked Lenny as they went inside.

"My mom's in the army," said Connor.

"Cool," said Lenny. "My dad's retired Marines."

"Want a snack?" asked Connor.

Lenny grinned. "As long as it's not rations! Those dried dinners are nasty!"

Connor laughed and tossed Lenny a bag of dried fruit. "This doesn't count, right?"

"Nope!" Lenny ate a handful.

"Who helps with your homework?" asked Lenny as the boys spread out their papers.

"Dad does," said Connor. "But I keep telling him I don't need help."

"So, what's homework today?" Connor's dad poked his head in.

The boys tried not to crack up.

"Since I'm a newbie," said Connor, "all we have to do is make a map of one of our rooms."

The boys high-fived.

When their maps were done, Lenny asked, "What do you do for fun?"
"When we lived on base," said Connor, "there was a cool obstacle
course. But we have a basketball hoop here. Want to play?"
"Sure," said Lenny.

"Who taught you how to shoot?" asked Lenny.

"My mom," said Connor.

"She played at West Point."

"Um, who gets your ball down?" asked Lenny.

Connor laughed. "I guess my dad. Dad!"

After Connor's dad got the ball down, Connor asked, "Want to learn some trick dribbles?" "Sure!" said Lenny.

Connor showed Lenny how to dribble under his leg. **Click!**

He showed him how to dribble behind his back. **Click!**

He even showed him how to spin the ball on his finger and then roll it around his neck. **Click!**

"Wow!" said Lenny.

"Dinner, Globetrotters!" called
Connor's dad.

"Who makes your dinner?" asked Lenny.
"My dad," said Connor. "Except when Mom
is home. Then she makes her famous
mac and cheese!"

Lenny scraped the last bit of sloppy joes off his plate.
"Who clears the dishes?" he asked.

Connor saluted. "Kitchen Patrol at your service!" **Click!**
"I have KP duty at home, too!" said Lenny.

"Can I see your room?" asked Lenny.
"Sure," said Connor.

"Awesome!" said Lenny.

"He shoots," said Connor, taking off
his socks, "he scores!" **Click!**

"Who does your laundry?" asked Lenny.
"My dad. The time Mom did it, she
turned our underwear PINK!"
Lenny fell down laughing as Connor
shook his head.

"Who reads your bedtime story?" asked Lenny.

Connor checked his watch. "Wait and see!"

"Lenny, your mom is here!" called Connor's dad as he walked in carrying a laptop.

"Time to go, Lenny," said his mom.

"One more minute?" asked Lenny.

"Sure," she said as the computer blinked on.

"Who reads your bedtime story?" asked Lenny again.

"Mom!" yelled Connor as his mom appeared on the screen. **Click!**

Lenny waved at the screen. "So who loves you best?"

"We do!" said Connor's parents. **Click!**

31

"See you at school, newbie!" said
Lenny as he tiptoed out of the room.
"You bet, oldie!" said Connor.